Daddy Has a Pair of Striped Shorts

Mimi Otey

Daddy Has a Pair of Striped Shorts

Farrar, Straus and Giroux
New York

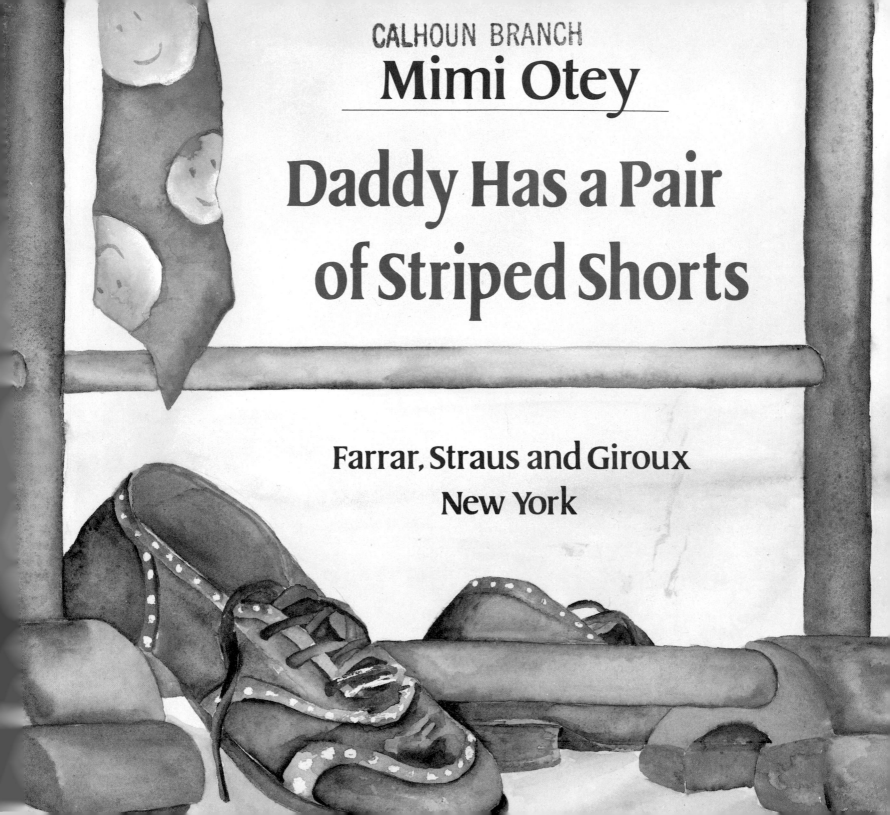

Daddy has a pair of striped shorts

that he wears with his Hawaiian shirt

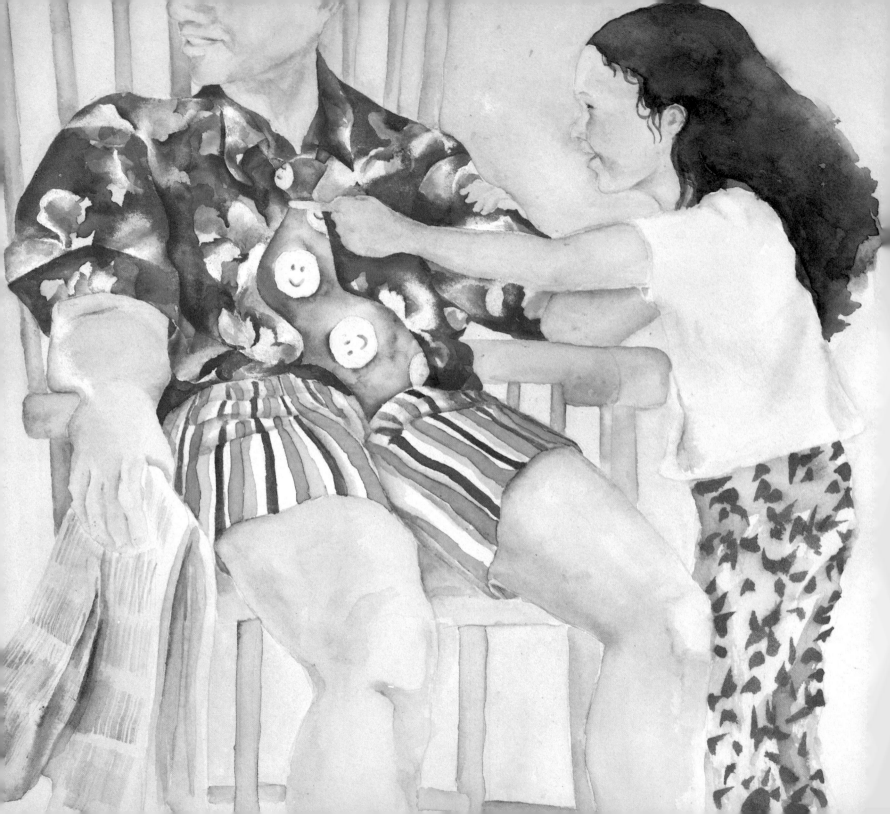

and his smiley-face tie.

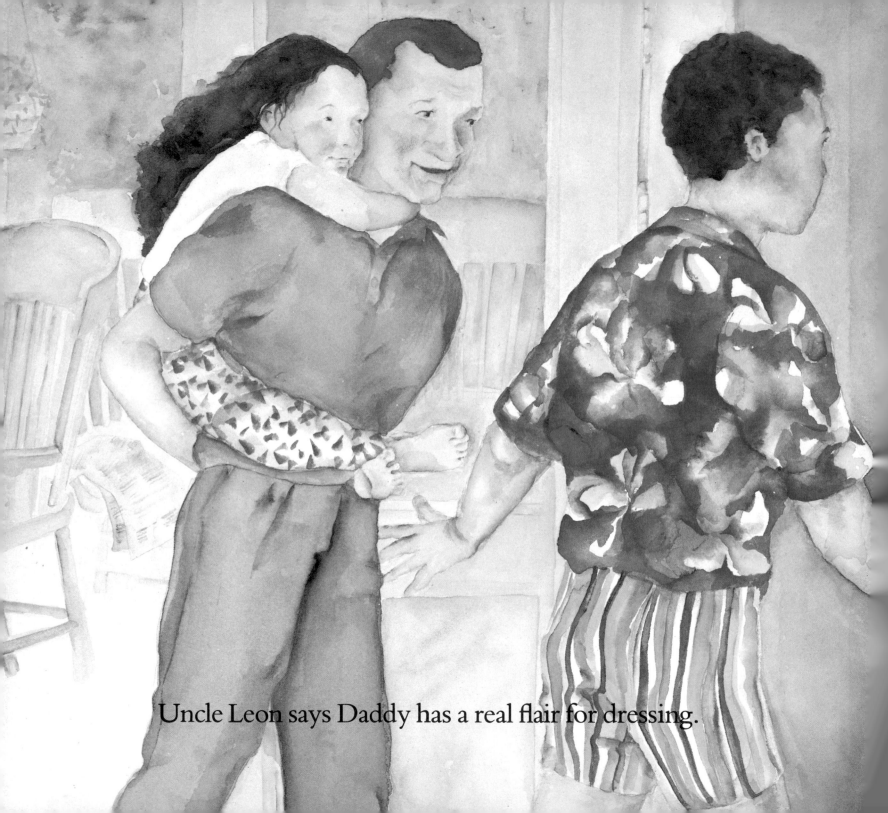

Uncle Leon says Daddy has a real flair for dressing.

Mama says that he is color-blind.

My brother John and I . . .we think he just has bad taste.

And sometimes it's embarrassing.

Daddy believes in supporting the PTA.

And he likes to know who our teachers are.

Daddy also believes in Sunday matinees,

and family night at Morrison's cafeteria.

Daddy thinks it's important to meet our new friends

and their parents.

POOL RULES
1. NO RUNNING
2. NO HORSEPLAYING
3. NO DUNKING
4. NO DIVING
BELOW 6 FEET

On Saturdays, he comes early to pick us up from swim class.

He always has lots to say about perfecting the butterfly stroke.

On top of all this,

Daddy is a preacher.

Once in a while, he manages to blend in.

But most of the time he just stands out.

Funny, how people seem to like him no matter what he wears

or how bright it is.

And now that I've been thinking about it,

so do I.